the
tree
in
me

Corinna Luyken

Dial Books
for Young Readers

The tree in me

is part apple,

part orange-pear-almond-plum

(part yummm),

part shade,

and part sun.

The tree in me
is seed and blossom,
bark and stump,

branch and trunk

and crown!

It is bird-squirrel-worm

and bee!

And because there is
a tree in me,

there is wind,

and rain,

and dirt,

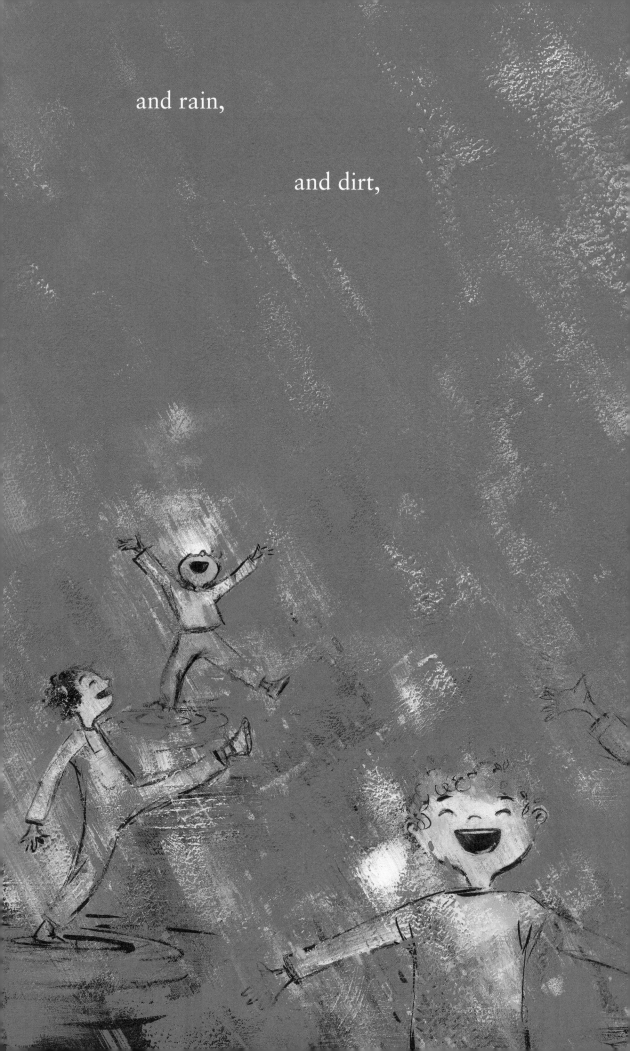

and a river with fish,

and a sky too.

The tree in me
is strong.

It bends,

and has roots
that go deep . . .

down to where
other roots reach up
toward their own
trunk-branch-crown

and sky too.

Because there is
a tree,
and a sky,
and a sun
in me,

I can see

that there is also
a tree . . .

in you.

For MacLeod and Quinn

Dial Books for Young Readers
An imprint of Penguin Random House LLC, New York

First published in the United States of America by Dial Books for Young Readers,
an imprint of Penguin Random House LLC, 2021

Copyright © 2021 by Corinna Luyken

Visit us online at penguinrandomhouse.com.

Library of Congress Cataloging-in-Publication Data is available.
Manufactured in China • ISBN 9780593112595

10 9 8 7 6 5 4 3 2 1

Design by Lily Malcom • Text set in Sabon

The art for this book was created using gouache, pencil, and ink.

*With gratitude to Steven Malk,
Lauri Hornik, and Lily Malcom*